This
Little Princess Story
belongs to:

. . . .

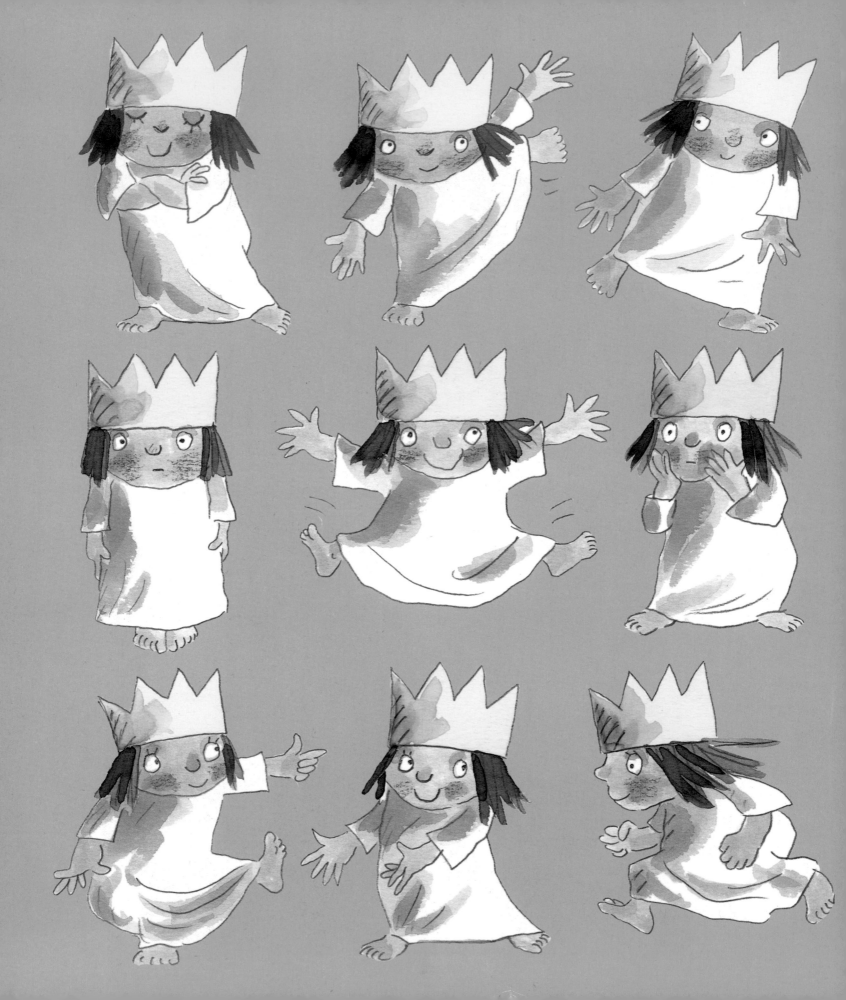

For Jackson Lee

This paperback edition published in 2012 by Andersen Press Ltd.
Published in Australia by Random House Australia Pty.,
Level 3, 100 Pacific Highway, North Sydney, NSW 2060.
First published in Great Britain in 2011 by Andersen Press Ltd.
Text and illustrations copyright © Tony Ross, 2011
The rights of Tony Ross to be identified as the author and illustrator
of this work have been asserted by him in accordance with
the Copyright, Designs and Patents Act, 1988.
All rights reserved.
Colour separated in Switzerland by Photolitho AG, Zürich.
Printed and bound in China by Foshan Zhao Rong Printing Co., Ltd.
Tony Ross has used pen, ink and watercolours in this book.

10   9   8   7   6   5   4   3   2

British Library Cataloguing in Publication Data available.
ISBN 978 1 84939 369 0 (Trade paperback edition)
ISBN 978 1 78344 028 3 (Riverside edition)

A Little Princess Story

I Want a Party!

Tony Ross

Andersen Press

The Little Princess was bored, bored, bored.
"I WANT A PARTY!" she said.

"But it isn't Christmas!" said her mother.
"I don't want a CHRISTMAS party," said the Little Princess.
"I just want a party."

"But it isn't your birthday!" said the King.
"I don't want a BIRTHDAY party," said the Little Princess.
"I just want a party."

So the Little Princess spent the rest of the week
writing lots of invitations to her party.

The Cook helped her make a party cake and
the wobbliest jelly in the world.

"Can I help?" asked the Prime Minister.
"Yes, please," said the Little Princess.
"You can help me make some party hats."

The General showed the Little Princess
how to play his favourite game.
"No peeping," he said. He knew she liked to cheat.

Every night, the Little Princess dreamed about her party. It was going to be the best party ever.

When the day of the party finally arrived, the Little Princess put on her favourite dress and her best crown.

The King helped her blow up the balloons . . .

the Queen put the finishing touches to the decorations . . .

and the Maid filled the party bags with lots of goodies.

At last, everything was ready for the great party . . .

. . . but nobody came. Nobody at all.

A tear rolled down the Little Princess's cheek.
"Why has nobody come to my party?" she sobbed.

Just then, someone knocked on the door.
The Little Princess rushed to open it.
There was only one person there. It was her best friend.

"Hello," said her best friend. "I am having a party next week, and I would like you to come. PLEASE come."
She held out an invitation to the Little Princess.

"Thank you, I would LOVE to come," said the Little Princess.
"Do come in. I have arranged a party, JUST FOR YOU!"

So the Little Princess and her best friend had a wonderful party.
If there is only one guest, it is good if it is your best friend.

And when the party ended, her best
friend left with LOTS of party bags.

"That was the best party EVER!"
said the Little Princess . . .

"... UNTIL, OF COURSE, NEXT WEEK!"

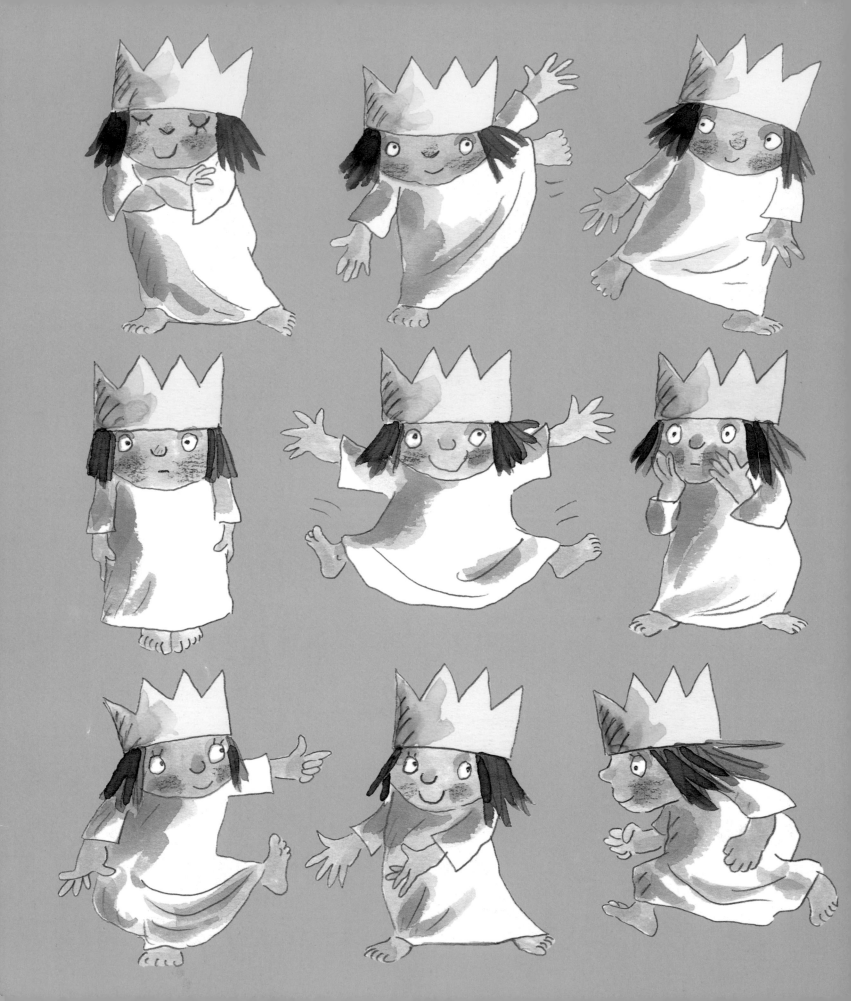

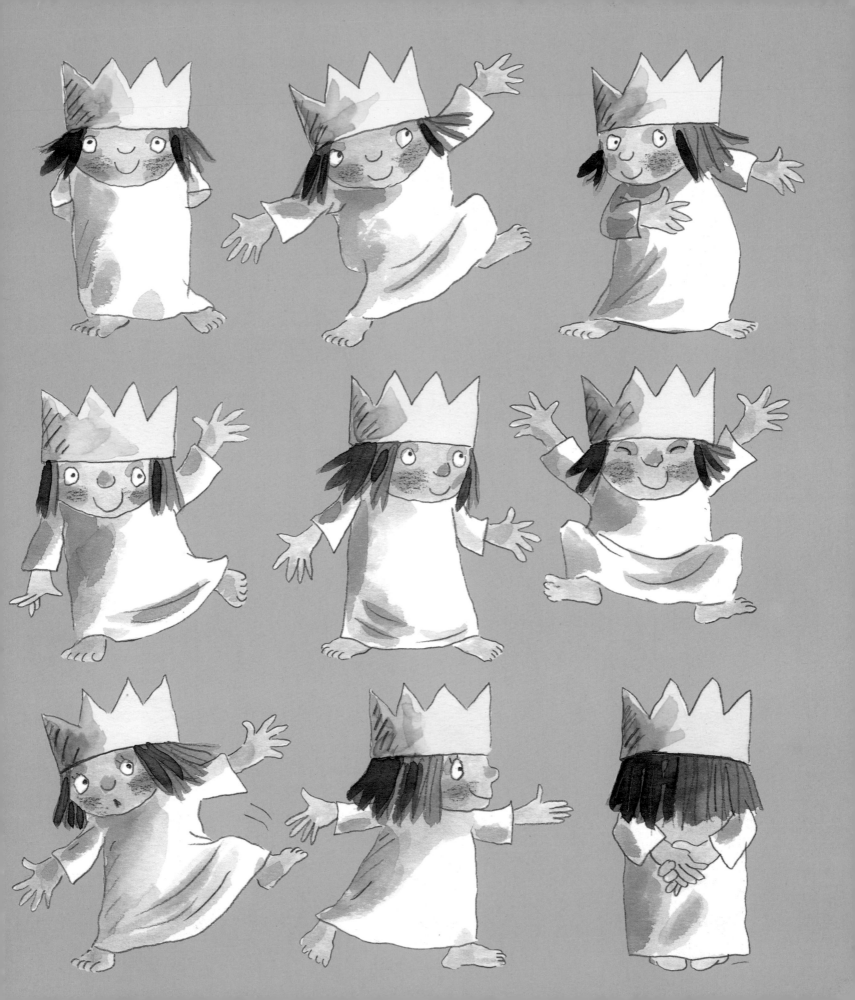

Other Little Princess Books

I Didn't Do it!

I Don't Want to Go to Hospital!

I Don't Want to Wash My Hands!

I Want a Boyfriend!

I Want a Party!

I Want a Sister!

I Want My Dummy!

I Want My Light On!

I Want My Potty!

I Want to Be!

I Want to Do it By Myself!

I Want to Go Home!

I Want to Win!

I Want Two Birthdays!

Little Princess titles are also available as eBooks.

LITTLE PRINCESS TV TIE-INS

Fun in the Sun!

I Want to Do Magic!

I Want My Sledge!

I Don't Like Salad!

I Don't Want to Comb My Hair!

I Want to Go to the Fair!

I Want to Be a Cavegirl!

I Want to Be Tall!

I Want My Sledge! Book and DVD